Story play™

This book belongs to

_____ .

This book was read by

_____

on

_____ .

Are you ready to start reading the **StoryPlay** way?

Read the story on its own. Play the activities together
as you read!

Ready. Set. Smart!

YOU CAN NEVER

RUN OUT OF LOVE

by Helen Docherty illustrated by Ali Pye

Cartwheel Books • An Imprint of Scholastic Inc.

First published in Great Britain in 2017 by Simon & Schuster UK Ltd. 1st Floor, 222 Gray's Inn Road, London WC1X8HB

Scholastic Inc., 557 Broadway, New York, NY 10012

Library of Congress Cataloging-in-Publication Data available

ISBN 978-1-338-21543-4

10 9 8 7 6 5 4 3 2 1   17 18 19 20 21

Printed in Panyu, China   137
This edition first printing, December 2017
Book design by Doan Buu

For Sally, Clara, and Alex; and for Bethan,
who inspired this story — HD

For Carol and Peter Nash — AP

You can run out of cookies

Or run out of bread.

You can run out of energy,

flopped on your bed.

How do you feel
when you run out
of energy?

You can run out of chocolates

(none left in this box).

When the laundry piles up,

you can run out
of socks.

You can run out of time . . .

You can run out
of money.

You can run out of patience,

Can you find the boy's broken kite?
What do you think happened to it?

when things don't seem funny. BUT . . .

You can never (no never, not ever),

Who do you think fixed the kite? Why?

you can never
run out of LOVE.

You can run out of milk.

Do you see MORE than or FEWER than 10 jars on the shelves? Are there MORE than or FEWER than 20?

You can run out of jelly.

If you run out of diapers,

things can get smelly!

You can run out of glue.

The girls have no glue left. How can they solve this problem?

You can run out of soap.

When you know it's too late,

The End

you can run out of hope.

On a very bad day, you can run out of luck . . . .

Or run out of ideas,

What do you think an idea is?
Can you think of one now?

and get really stuck. BUT . . .

You can never (no never, not ever),

you can never
run out of LOVE.

Love doesn't come
in a bottle or jar.

You don't have to charge it.
No batteries inside.

Your love can be BIG,
as the whole world is wide.

You can't measure love in a bucket or cup.

You don't have to worry you'll use it all up.

'Cause love's not a game where you have to keep score.

Whenever you give some,

you'll always have more.

When you've run out of everything else,

you'll still find . . .

Can you find the people who are dancing?
What about the person playing guitar? Do you see
the woman holding a baby? Point to each one.

you can never
run out of LOVE.

What are some things you do
to express YOUR love?

Story time fun never ends with these creative activities!

★ I Spy ★

The characters in the story have pets that are with them on almost every page. The little girls have a black cat. The little boy has a bunny and a dog. Did you spot them in the background? Flip through the book and see if you can find each of the pictures below!

I Spy . . .

- A cat playing with a red bow
- A bunny in a basket
- A dog taking a bath
- A cat visiting the doctor
- A bunny with a medal
- A dog eating homework

★ I Love You! ★

Families come in all shapes and sizes — but all of them are full of love! Draw a picture of you with the people you love. What do you love about them? Don't forget to add your name to your picture!